Happily Ever After

Happily Ever After

a book lover's treasury of
happy endings

COMPILED BY WALTER BROWDER

RUTLEDGE HILL PRESS
Nashville, Tennessee
A Division of Thomas Nelson Publishers
Since 1798

www.thomasnelson.com

Published by Rutledge Hill Press, a Division of Thomas Nelson, Inc.,
P.O. Box 141000, Nashville, Tennessee 37214.

Pages 133–138 constitute an extension of this copyright page.

Rutledge Hill Press books may be purchased in bulk for educational, business,
fundraising, or sales promotional use. For information, please e-mail
SpecialMarkets@ThomasNelson.com.

Library of Congress Cataloging-in-Publication Data

Happily ever after : a book lover's treasury of happy endings / compiled by Walter
Browder.

    p. cm.

    ISBN 1-4016-0213-4 (hardcover)

    1. Quotations, English. 2. Closure (Rhetoric) 3. Happiness in literature.

I. Browder, Walter, 1939–

    PN6084.C534H36 2005

    808.8—dc22

2005000894

Printed in the United States of America

05 06 07 08 09 — 9 8 7 6 5 4 3 2 1

For Dustin Browder

... but the one overpowering fact, ... ntured to deal with poetry,

THE END

∾ *Preface* ∾

It's been said there are no happy endings. But in troubling times it's good to remind ourselves that the human spirit has endured many dark hours, that love runs deeper than fear, and that our best culture makers have always believed in happy and optimistic endings. It's been said we live in an age when all will end in despair. But the greatest storytellers and dreamers have always held out hope for tomorrow. And they have always written endings that tell of that hope. What follows is an inspiring collection of happy and optimistic endings from the world's best writers. Read them and smile. As William Shakespeare so aptly put it, "All's well that ends well."

*A*unt Em had just come out of the house to water the cabbages when she looked up and saw Dorothy running toward her.

"My darling child!" she cried, folding the little girl in her arms and covering her face with kisses. "Where in the world did you come from?"

"From the Land of Oz," said Dorothy gravely. "And here is Toto, too. And oh, Aunt Em! I'm so glad to be at home again!"

—L. FRANK BAUM, *THE WIZARD OF OZ*

$\mathcal{S}$crooge was better than his word. He did it all, and infinitely more; and to Tiny Tim, who did NOT die, he was a second father. He became as good a friend, as good a master, and as good a man, as the good old city knew, or any other good old city, town, or borough, in the good old world. Some people laughed to see the alteration in him, but he let them laugh, and little heeded them; for he was wise enough to know that nothing ever happened on this globe, for good, at which some people did not have their fill of laughter in the outset; and knowing that such as these would be blind anyway, he thought it was as well that they should wrinkle up their eyes in grins, as have the malady in less attractive forms. His own heart laughed; and that was quite enough for him.

He had no further intercourse with Spirits, but lived upon the Total Abstinence Principle, ever afterwards; and it was always said of him, that he knew how to keep Christmas well, if any man alive possessed the knowledge. May that be truly said of us, and all of us! And so, as Tiny Tim observed, God bless Us, Every One!

—CHARLES DICKENS, *A CHRISTMAS CAROL*

"*You* are a very fine person, Mr. Baggins, and I am very fond of you; but you are only quite a little fellow in a wide world after all!"

"Thank goodness!" said Bilbo laughing, and handed him the tobacco-jar.

—J. R. R. TOLKIEN, *THE HOBBIT*

*L*aura lay awake a little while, listening to Pa's fiddle softly playing and to the lonely sound of the wind in the Big Woods. She looked at Pa sitting on the bench by the hearth, the fire-light gleaming on his brown hair and beard and glistening on the honey-brown fiddle. She looked at Ma, gently rocking and knitting.

She thought to herself, "This is now."

She was glad that the cosy house, and Pa and Ma and the fire-light and the music, were now. They could not be forgotten, she thought, because now is now. It can never be a long time ago.

—LAURA INGALLS WILDER, *LITTLE HOUSE IN THE BIG WOODS*

My sisters and I stand, arms around each other, laughing and wiping the tears from each other's eyes. The flash of the Polaroid goes off and my father hands me the snapshot. My sisters and I watch quietly together, eager to see what develops.

The gray-green surface changes to the bright colors of our three images, sharpening and deepening all at once. And although we don't speak, I know we all see it: Together we look like our mother. Her same eyes, her same mouth, open in surprise to see, at last, her long-cherished wish.

—AMY TAN, *THE JOY LUCK CLUB*

*P*hileas Fogg had won his wager, and had made his journey around the world in eighty days. To do this he had employed every means of conveyance—steamers, railways, carriages, yachts, trading-vessels, sledges, elephants. The eccentric gentleman had throughout displayed all his marvellous qualities of coolness and exactitude. But what then? What had he really gained by all this trouble? What had he brought back from this long and weary journey?

Nothing, say you? Perhaps so; nothing but a charming woman, who, strange as it may appear, made him the happiest of men!

Truly, would you not for less than that make the tour around the world?

—JULES VERNE, *AROUND THE WORLD IN 80 DAYS*

"Yes, Jo, I think your harvest will be a good one," began Mrs. March, frightening away a big black cricket that was staring Teddy out of countenance.

"Not half so good as yours, mother. Here it is, and we never can thank you enough for the patient sowing and reaping you have done," cried Jo, with the loving impetuosity which she never could outgrow.

"I hope there will be more wheat and fewer tares every year," said Amy softly.

"A large sheaf, but I know there's room in your heart for it, Marmee dear," added Meg's tender voice.

Touched to the heart, Mrs. March could only stretch out her arms, as if to gather children and grandchildren to herself, and say, with face and voice full of motherly love, gratitude, and humility—

"O my girls, however long you may live, I never can wish you a greater happiness than this!"

—LOUISA MAY ALCOTT, LITTLE WOMEN

$\mathcal{W}$e climb the ladder and Tim calls to us from his little boat, Mind yourselves going up that ladder. Oh, boys, oh, boys, wasn't that a grand night? Good night, boys, and good night, Father.

We watch his little boat till it disappears into the dark of the Poughkeepsie riverbank. The priest says good night and goes below and the First Officer follows him.

I stand on the deck with the Wireless Officer looking at the lights of America twinkling. He says, My God, that was a lovely night, Frank. Isn't this a great country altogether?

—FRANK MCCOURT, *ANGELA'S ASHES: A MEMOIR*

$\mathcal{W}$illie always speaks to me when he can, and treats me as his special friend. My ladies have promised that I shall never be sold, and so I have nothing to fear; and here my story ends. My troubles are all over, and I am at home; and often before I am quite awake, I fancy I am still in the orchard at Birtwick standing with my old friends under the apple trees.

—ANNA SEWELL, BLACK BEAUTY

*T*he eyes of both were fixed upon the spot indicated by the sailor, and on the blue line separating the sky from the Mediterranean Sea they perceived a large white sail.

"Gone!" said Morrel; "gone!—Adieu, my friend!—adieu, my father!"

"Gone!" murmured Valentine: "adieu, my friend!—adieu, my sister!"

"Who can say whether we shall ever see them again?" said Morrel, with tearful eyes.

"Darling," replied Valentine, "has not the count just told us that all human wisdom is contained in the words,— *'Wait and hope'* ?"

—ALEXANDER DUMAS, *THE COUNT OF MONTE CRISTO*

But what a lucky man. Some luck lies in not getting what you thought you wanted but getting what you have, which once you have it you may be smart enough to see is what you would have wanted had you known. He takes deep breaths and the cold air goes to his brain and makes him more sensible. He starts out on the short walk to the house where people love him and will be happy to see his face.

—GARRISON KEILLOR, *LAKE WOBEGON DAYS*

"But we don't know where Jeremy is, either. We don't see the crows down here," Mrs. Frisby reminded him.

"No, but in the fall, when we go back to the garden—I could find him then. If I got something shiny and put it out in the sun, he'd come to get it." Martin was growing excited at his idea. "Oh, Mother, *may* I?"

"I don't know. I doubt that the rats will want visitors from the outside."

"They wouldn't mind. After all, you helped them, and so did Father. And I wouldn't do any harm."

"It's not something we have to decide tonight," said Mrs. Frisby. "I'll think about it. And now it's late. It's time for bed."

The sun had set. They went into the house and lay down on the soft moss Mrs. Frisby had placed on the floor of their room under the roots. Outside, the brook swam quietly through the woods, and up above them the warm wind blew through the newly opened leaves of the big oak tree. They went to sleep.

—ROBERT C. O'BRIEN, *MRS. FRISBY AND THE RATS OF NIMH*

$\mathcal{A}$t the end of every song she was back beside me. And together under the arches of many arms Juliet and I sashayed, danced lively down the line to the tune as it swelled—accordion, fiddles and flute—danced lively as the music lifted up through the trees, out over the lake, and into the deep blue night.

—BILL ROORBACH, *SUMMERS WITH JULIET*

*J*udge Henry at Sunk Creek had his wedding present ready. His growing affairs in Wyoming needed his presence in many places distant from his ranch, and he made the Virginian his partner. When the thieves prevailed at length, as they did, forcing cattle owners to leave the country or be ruined, the Virginian had forestalled this crash. The herds were driven away to Montana. Then, in 1892, came the cattle war, when, after putting their men in office, and coming to own some of the newspapers, the thieves brought ruin on themselves as well. For in a broken country there is nothing left to steal.

But the railroad came, and built a branch to that land of the Virginian's where the coal was. By that time he was an important man, with a strong grip on many various enterprises, and able to give his wife all and more than she asked or desired. Sometimes she missed the Bear Creek days, when she and he had ridden together, and sometimes she declared that his work would kill him. But it does not seem to have done so. Their eldest boy rides the horse Monte; and, strictly between ourselves, I think his father is going to live a long while.

—OWEN WISTER, *THE VIRGINIAN*

*O*n the pond where the swans were, Louis put his trumpet away. The cygnets crept under their mother's wings. Darkness settled on woods and fields and marsh. A loon called its wild night cry. As Louis relaxed and prepared for sleep, all his thoughts were of how lucky he was to inhabit such a beautiful earth, how lucky he had been to solve his problems with music, and how pleasant it was to look forward to another night of sleep and another day tomorrow, and the fresh morning, and the light that returns with the day.

—E. B. WHITE, *THE TRUMPET OF THE SWAN*

Schopenhauer said happiness is a negative state—but I disagree. For the last twenty years I have known what happiness means. I have the good fortune to be married to a wonderful wife. I wish I could write more about this, but it involves love, and perfect love is the most beautiful of all frustrations because it is more than one can express. As I live with Oona, the depth and beauty of her character are a continual revelation to me. Even as she walks ahead of me along the narrow sidewalks of Vevey with simple dignity, her neat little figure straight, her dark hair smoothed back showing a few silver threads, a sudden wave of love and admiration comes over me for all that she is—and a lump comes into my throat.

With such happiness, I sometimes sit out on our terrace at sunset and look over a vast green lawn to the lake in the distance, and beyond the lake to the reassuring mountains, and in this mood think of nothing and enjoy their magnificent serenity.

—CHARLES CHAPLIN, *MY AUTOBIOGRAPHY*

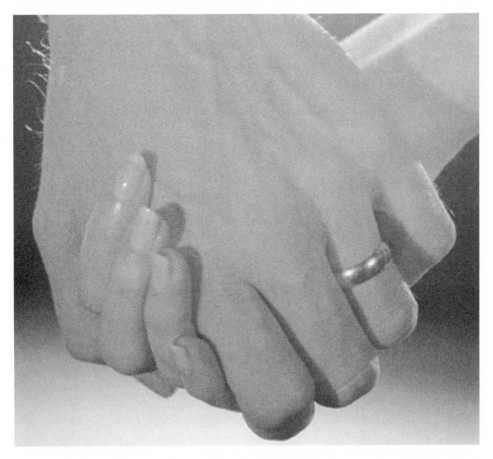

$\mathcal{M}$arion said, "Oh, I feel terrible about not paying you anything. Won't you let me give you a little something, at least?"

The old woman shook her head. "No, it's free. You won it, fair and square. You don't know this, but your little girl, here, just happens to be my one millionth customer this month."

"I AM?"

"That's right, my one millionth."

Marion smiled at the old woman. "Well, if you insist. Patsy, what do you say?"

"Thank you."

"You're welcome. And listen, Patsy, if you ever get anywhere around these parts again, you be sure and look me up, y'hear?"

"Yes ma'am, I will."

As they pulled out, Bill tooted his horn and the little girl waved goodbye.

The old woman stood on the side of the road and waved back until the car was out of sight.

—FANNIE FLAGG, FRIED GREEN TOMATOES AT THE WHISTLE STOP CAFE

*N*ight has closed around me.

For the last time my united family slumbers beneath my care.

Tomorrow this closing chapter of my journey will pass into the hands of my eldest son.

From afar I greet thee, Europe!

I greet thee, dear old Switzerland!

Like thee, may New Switzerland flourish and prosper—good, happy, and free!

—JOHANN WYSS, *THE SWISS FAMILY ROBINSON*

The sacred contents of that box are a parent's pure love for a child, manifested first by a Father's love for all His children, as He sacrificed that which He loved most and sent His son to earth on that Christmas day so long ago. And as long as the earth lives, and longer, that message will never die. Though the cold winds of life may put a frost on the heart of many, that message alone will shelter the heart from life's storms. And for me, as long as I live, the magic inside the Christmas Box will never die.

It never will.

—RICHARD PAUL EVANS, *THE CHRISTMAS BOX*

*T*he result of this distress was that with a much more voluntary, cheerful consent than his daughter had ever presumed to hope for at the moment, she was able to fix her wedding-day; and Mr. Elton was called on, within a month from the marriage of Mr. and Mrs. Robert Martin, to join the hands of Mr. Knightley and Miss Woodhouse.

The wedding was very much like other weddings where the parties have no taste for finery or parade; and Mrs. Elton, from the particulars detailed by her husband, thought it all extremely shabby and very inferior to her own. "Very little white satin, very few lace veils; a most pitiful business! Selina would stare when she heard of it." But in spite of these deficiencies, the wishes, the hopes, the confidence, the predictions of the small band of true friends who witnessed the ceremony, were fully answered in the perfect happiness of the union.

—JANE AUSTEN, *EMMA*

The story of Hans Brinker would be but half told, if we did not leave him with Gretel standing near. Dear, quick, patient little Gretel! What is she now? Ask old Dr. Boekman, he will declare she is the finest singer, the loveliest woman in Amsterdam; ask Hans and Annie, they will assure you she is the dearest sister ever known; ask her husband, he will tell you she is the brightest, sweetest little wife in Holland; ask Dame Brinker and Raff, their eyes will glisten with joyous tears; ask the poor, the air will be filled with blessings.

But, lest you forget a tiny form trembling and sobbing on the mound before the Brinker cottage, ask the Van Glecks; they will never weary telling of the darling little girl who won the silver skates.

—MARY MAPES DODGE, *HANS BRINKER, OR THE SILVER SKATES*

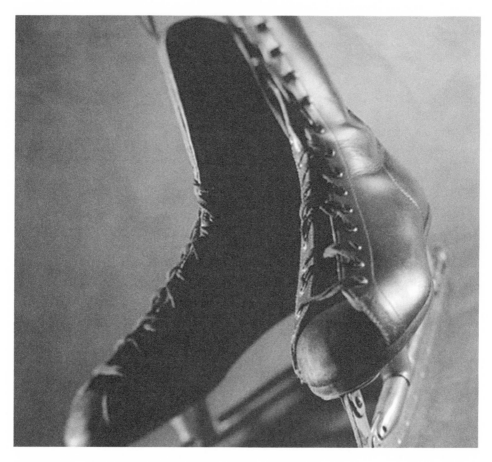

*T*hroughout my childhood I had the good fortune to savor the delicious fruits and vegetables that grew on that land. Eventually my mother had a little apartment building built there. My father Alex still lives in one of the apartments. Today he is going to come to my house to celebrate my birthday. That is why I am preparing Christmas Rolls, my favorite dish. My mama prepared them for me every year. My mama! . . . How wonderful the flavor, the aroma of her kitchen, her stories as she prepared the meal, her Christmas Rolls! I don't know why mine never turn out like hers, or why my tears flow so freely when I prepare them—perhaps I am as sensitive to onions as Tita, my great-aunt, who will go on living as long as there is someone who cooks her recipes.

—LAURA ESQUIVEL, *LIKE WATER FOR CHOCOLATE*

"I will tell you. The Romans, even this Nero, hold two things sacred—I know of no others they so hold—they are the ashes of the dead and all places of burial. If you can not build temples for the worship of the Lord above ground, then build them below the ground; and to keep them from profanation, carry to them the bodies of all who die in the faith."

Ben-Hur arose excitedly.

"It is a great idea," he said. "I will not wait to begin it. Time forbids waiting. The ship that brought the news of the suffering of our brethren shall take me to Rome. I will sail to-morrow."

He turned to Malluch.

"Get the ship ready, Malluch, and be thou ready to go with me."

"It is well," said Simonides.

"And thou, Esther, what sayest thou?" asked Ben-Hur.

Esther came to his side, and put her hand on his arm, and answered,

"So wilt thou best serve the Christ. O my husband, let me not hinder, but go with thee and help."

If any of my readers, visiting Rome, will make the short journey to the Catacomb of San Calixto, which is more ancient than that of San Sebastiano, he will see what became of the fortune of Ben-Hur, and give him thanks. Out of that vast tomb Christianity issued to supersede the Caesars.

—LEW WALLACE, *BEN-HUR: A TALE OF THE CHRIST*

"*I* wonder where the old Pinocchio of wood has hidden himself?"

"There he is," answered Geppetto. And he pointed to a large Marionette leaning against a chair, head turned to one side, arms hanging limp, and legs twisted under him.

After a long, long look, Pinocchio said to himself with great content:

"How ridiculous I was as a Marionette! And how happy I am, now that I have become a real boy!"

—CARLO COLLODI, *THE ADVENTURES OF PINOCCHIO*
(TRANSLATED BY M. A. MURRAY)

*Y*es, it is the dawn that has come. The titihoya wakes from sleep, and goes about its work of forlorn crying. The sun tips with light the mountains of Ingeli and East Griqualand. The great valley of the Umzimkulu is still in darkness, but the light will come there. Ndotsheni is still in darkness, but the light will come there also. For it is the dawn that has to come, as it has come for a thousand centuries, never failing. But when that dawn will come, of our emancipation, from the fear of bondage and the bondage of fear, why, that is a secret.

—ALAN PATON, CRY, THE BELOVED COUNTRY

*I*t was two weeks before Lad could stand upright, and two more before he could go out of doors unhelped. Then on a warm, early spring morning, the vet declared him out of all danger.

Very thin was the invalid, very shaky, snow-white of muzzle and with the air of an old, old man whose too-fragile body is sustained only by a regal dignity. But he was *alive.*

Slowly he marched from his piano cave toward the open front door. Wolf—in black disgrace for the past month—chanced to be crossing the living room toward the veranda at the same time. The two dogs reached the doorway simultaneously.

Very respectfully, almost cringingly, Wolf stood aside for Lad to pass out.

His sire walked by with never a look. But his step was all at once stronger and springier, and he held his splendid head high.

For Lad knew he was still king!

—ALBERT PAYSON TERHUNE, *LAD: A DOG*

*D*ouglas in the high cupola above the town, moved his hand.

"Everyone, clothes off!"

He waited. The wind blew, icing the windowpane.

"Brush teeth."

He waited again.

"Now," he said at last, "out with the lights!"

He blinked. And the town winked out its lights, sleepily, here, there, as the courthouse clock struck ten, ten-thirty, eleven, and drowsy midnight.

"The last one now . . . there . . . there . . ."

He lay in his bed and the town slept around him and the ravine was dark and the lake was moving quietly on its shore and everyone, his family, his friends, the old people and the young, slept on one street or another, in one house or another, or slept in the far country churchyards.

He shut his eyes.

June dawns, July noons, August evenings over, finished, done, and gone forever with only the sense of it all left here in his head. Now, a whole autumn, a white winter, a cool and greening spring to figure sums and totals of summer past. And if he should forget, the dandelion wine stood in the cellar, numbered huge for each and every day. He would go there often, stare straight into the sun until he could stare no more, then close his eyes and consider the burned spots, the fleeting scars left dancing on his warm eyelids; arranging, rearranging each fire and reflection until the pattern was clear. . . .

So thinking, he slept.

And, sleeping, put an end to Summer, 1928.

—RAY BRADBURY, *DANDELION WINE*

The youth smiled, for he saw that the world was a world for him, though many discovered it to be made of oaths and walking sticks. He had rid himself of the red sickness of battle. The sultry nightmare was in the past. He had been an animal blistered and sweating in the heat and pain of war. He turned now with a lover's thirst to images of tranquil skies, fresh meadows, cool brooks—an existence of soft and eternal peace.

Over the river a golden ray of sun came through the hosts of leaden rain clouds.

—STEPHEN CRANE, *THE RED BADGE OF COURAGE*

It was home; her roof, her garden, her green acres, her dear trees; it was shelter for the little family at Sunnybrook; her mother would have once more the companionship of her sister and the friends of her girlhood; the children would have teachers and playmates.

And she? Her own future was close-folded still; folded and hidden in beautiful mists; but she leaned her head against the sun-warmed door, and closing her eyes, whispered, just as if she had been a child saying her prayers: "God bless Aunt Miranda; God bless the brick house that was; God bless the brick house that is to be!"

—KATE DOUGLAS WIGGIN, *REBECCA OF SUNNYBROOK FARM*

"Are you listening to all that?" Thorne said. "I wouldn't take any of it too seriously. It's just theories. Human beings can't help making them, but the fact is that theories are just fantasies. And they change. When America was a new country, people believed in something called phlogiston. You know what that is? No? Well, it doesn't matter, because it wasn't real anyway. They also believed that four humors controlled behavior. And they believed that the earth was only a few thousand years old. Now we believe the earth is four billion years old, and we believe in photons and electrons, and we think human behavior is controlled by things like ego and self-esteem. We think those beliefs are more scientific and better."

"Aren't they?"

Thorne shrugged. "They're still just fantasies. They're not real. Have you ever seen a self-esteem? Can you bring me one on a plate? How about a photon? Can you bring me one of those?"

Kelly shook her head. "No, but . . ."

"And you never will, because those things don't exist. No matter how seriously people take them," Thorne said. "A hundred years from now, people will look back at us and laugh. They'll say, 'You know what people used to believe? They believed in photons and electrons. Can you imagine anything so silly?' They'll have a good laugh, because by then there will be newer and better fantasies." Thorne shook his head. "And meanwhile, you feel the way the boat moves? That's the sea. That's real. You smell the salt in the air? You feel the sunlight on your skin? That's all real. You see all of us together? That's real. Life is wonderful. It's a gift to be alive, to see the sun and breathe the air. And there isn't really anything else. Now look at that compass, and tell me where south is. I want to go to Puerto Cortés. It's time for us all to go home.

—MICHAEL CRICHTON, *THE LOST WORLD*

*T*om Davenport is now in the city, but his course is far from creditable. His father has more than once been compelled to pay his debts, and has angrily refused to do so again. In fact, he has lost a large part of his once handsome fortune, and bids fair to close his life in penury. Success has come to Ben because he deserved it, and well-merited retribution to Tom Davenport. Harvey Dinsmore, once given over to evil courses, has redeemed himself, and is a reputable business man in New York. Mrs. Hamilton still lives, happy in the success of her protégé. Conrad and his mother have tried more than once to regain their positions in her household, but in vain. None of my young readers will pity them. They are fully rewarded for their treachery.

—HORATIO ALGER, *THE STORE BOY;*
OR *THE FORTUNES OF BEN BARCLAY*

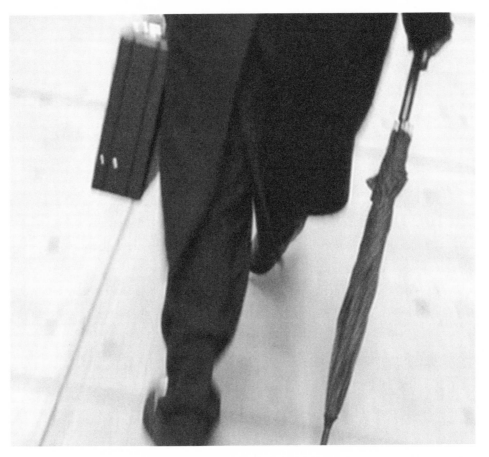

$\mathcal{L}$uther himself was lucky to be standing, as opposed to lying peacefully on a slab at Franklin's Funeral Home, or pinned to a bed in ICU at Mercy Hospital, tubes running everywhere. Thoughts of snowballing down his roof, head-first, still horrified him. Very lucky indeed.

Blessed with friends and neighbors who would sacrifice their plans for Christmas Eve to rescue him.

He looked up to his chimney where the Brixleys' Frosty was watching him. Round smiling face, top hat, corncob pipe. Through the flurries Luther thought he caught a wink from the snowman.

Starving, as usual, Luther suddenly craved smoked trout. He began trekking through the snow. "I'll eat a fruitcake too," he vowed to himself.

Skipping Christmas. What a ridiculous idea.

Maybe next year.

—JOHN GRISHAM, SKIPPING CHRISTMAS

$\mathcal{G}$eneral Moreno's name was still held in warm remembrance in the city of Mexico, and Felipe found himself at once among friends. On the day after their arrival he and Ramona were married in the cathedral, old Marda and Juan Can, with his crutches, kneeling in proud joy behind them. The story of the romance of their lives, being widely rumored, greatly enhanced the interest with which they were welcomed. The beautiful young Señora Moreno was the theme of the city; and Felipe's bosom thrilled with pride to see the gentle dignity of demeanor by which she was distinguished in all assemblages. It was indeed a new world, a new life. Ramona might well doubt her own identity. But undying memories stood like sentinels in her breast. When the notes of doves, calling to each other, fell on her ear, her eyes sought the sky, and she heard a voice saying, "Majella!" This was the only secret her loyal, loving heart had kept from Felipe. A loyal, loving heart indeed it was,—loyal, loving, serene. Few husbands so blest as the Señor Felipe Moreno.

Sons and daughters came to bear his name. The daughters were all beautiful; but the most beautiful of them all, and, it was said, the most beloved by both father and mother, was the eldest one: the one who bore the mother's name, and was only step-daughter to the Señor,— Ramona,—Ramona, daughter of Alessandro the Indian.

—HELEN HUNT JACKSON, RAMONA

*T*hen the sheriff he nabbed Brace Dunlap and his crowd, and by and by next month the judge had them up for trial and jailed the whole lot. And everybody crowded back to Uncle Silas's little old church, and was ever so loving and kind to him and the family and couldn't do enough for them; and Uncle Silas he preached them the blamedest jumbledest idiotic sermons you ever struck, and would tangle you up so you couldn't find your way home in daylight; but the people never let on but what they thought it was the clearest and brightest and elegantest sermons that ever was; and they would set there and cry, for love and pity; but, by George, they give me the jimjams and the fantods and caked up what brains I had, and turned them solid; but by and by they loved the old man's intellects back into him again, and he was as sound in his skull as ever he was, which ain't no flattery, I reckon. And so the whole family was as happy as birds, and nobody could be gratefuler and lovinger than what they was to Tom Sawyer; and the same to me, though I hadn't done nothing. And when the two thousand dollars come, Tom give half of it to me, and never told anybody so, which didn't surprise me, because I knowed him.

—MARK TWAIN, *TOM SAWYER*

"But it did really move? You're sure? You really felt it move?"

"Oh, yes. It moved."

For a long time he remained kneeling there, his head pressed against the softness of her belly. She clasped her hands behind his head and pulled it closer. He could hear nothing, only the blood drumming in his own ear. But she could not have been mistaken. Somewhere in there, in the safe, warm, cushioned darkness, it was alive and stirring.

Well, once again things were happening in the Comstock family.

—GEORGE ORWELL, *KEEP THE ASPIDISTRA FLYING*

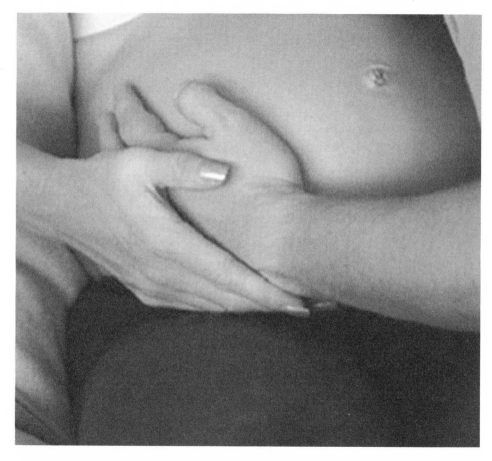

"Karamazov, we love you!" a voice, probably Kartashov's, cried impulsively.

"We love you, we love you!" they all caught it up. There were tears in the eyes of many of them.

"Hurrah for Karamazov!" Kolya shouted ecstatically.

"And may the dear boy's memory live for ever!" Alyosha added again with feeling.

"For ever!" the boys chimed in again.

"Karamazov," cried Kolya, "can it be true what's taught us in religion, that we shall all rise again from the dead and shall live and see each other again, all, Ilusha too?"

"Certainly we shall all rise again, certainly we shall see each other and shall tell each other with joy and gladness all that has happened!" Alyosha answered, half laughing, half enthusiastic.

"Ah, how splendid it will be!" broke from Kolya.

"Well, now we will finish talking and go to his funeral dinner. Don't be put out at our eating pancakes—it's a very old custom and there's something nice in that!" laughed Alyosha. "Well, let us go! And now we go hand in hand."

"And always so, all our lives hand in hand! Hurrah for Karamazov!" Kolya cried once more rapturously and once more the boys took up his exclamation:

"Hurrah for Karamazov!"

—FYODOR DOSTOYEVSKY, *THE BROTHERS KARAMAZOV*
(TRANSLATED BY CONSTANCE GARNETT)

$\mathcal{Y}$es, I thought, there is a whole 'nother world out there, and I would see it.

Late in the night, I looked out at the strange, flat land, and I could hear a train whistle blowing. The amazing thing was I was on that train. I thought of old Buddy and Daddy, my friends and teachers, Poppy, and, most of all, Lou Jean. Then I slept and dreamed I could hear Sweet Creek rippling over the rocks outside my bedroom window. And in her ripple I heard the long-ago, the lost, the far echo of laughter—the laughter of little girls running in the sunshine of another time, unafraid.

—RUTH WHITE, *SWEET CREEK HOLLER*

*H*e sat at the folding table in the basement, pondering what Miriam had said. How he'd been discouraged when God didn't seem to be working, then when God did do something it made him mad. It occurred to Sam that he wasn't an easy man to please.

Upstairs, the Frieda Hampton Memorial Clock bonged nine times. He rose from his chair, rinsed his coffee cup out in the kitchen sink, turned off the church lights, and walked down Main Street toward home.

Over at the Legal Grounds, Deena Morrison was turning the sign from *Yes, We're Open* to *Sorry, We're Closed.* She waved through the glass at Sam as he passed. He smiled and waved back.

She cracked open the door. "Have you heard the news about Sally?"

"Yes."

"Isn't God good," Deena said. It was a declaration, not a question.

Sam smiled and nodded his head in agreement.

God is good, he thought. Bewildering, but good.

—PHILIP GULLEY, *JUST SHY OF HARMONY*

$\mathcal{A}$nd how much there was to tell of all the events that had taken place that last summer, for they had not had many opportunities of meeting since then.

And it was difficult to say which of the three looked the happiest at being together again, and at the recollection of all the wonderful things that had happened. Mother Brigitta's face was perhaps the happiest of all, as now, with the help of Heidi's explanation, she was able to understand for the first time the history of Peter's weekly penny for life.

Then at last the grandmother spoke, "Heidi, read me one of the hymns! I feel I can do nothing for the remainder of my life but thank the Father in Heaven for all the mercies He has shown us!"

—JOHANNA SPYRI, HEIDI

"*I* wonder if you'll marry me, Sally."

She did not move and there was no flicker of emotion on her face, but she did not look at him when she answered.

"If you like."

"Don't you want to?"

"Oh, of course I'd like to have a house of my own, and it's about time I was settling down."

He smiled a little. He knew her pretty well by now, and her manner did not surprise him.

"But don't you want to marry *me?*"

"There's no one else I would marry."

"Then that settles it."

"Mother and Dad will be surprised, won't they?"

"I'm so happy."

"I want my lunch," she said.

"Dear!"

He smiled and took her hand and pressed it. They got up and walked out of the gallery. They stood for a moment at the balustrade

and looked at Trafalgar Square. Cabs and omnibuses hurried to and fro, and crowds passed, hastening in every direction, and the sun was shining.

—W. SOMERSET MAUGHAM, *OF HUMAN BONDAGE*

*F*letcher sighed and started over. "Hm. Ah . . . very well," he said, and eyed them critically. "Let's begin with Level Flight." And saying that, he understood all at once that his friend had quite honestly been no more divine than Fletcher himself.

No limits, Jonathan? he thought. Well, then, the time's not distant when I'm going to appear out of thin air on *your* beach, and show you a thing or two about flying!

And though he tried to look properly severe for his students, Fletcher Seagull suddenly saw them all as they really were, just for a moment, and he more than liked, he loved what it was he saw. No limits, Jonathan? he thought, and he smiled. His race to learn had begun.

—RICHARD BACH, *JONATHAN LIVINGSTON SEAGULL*

$\mathcal{A}$s I walked across that stage I felt something growing within me, something powerful, deeply committed, and unfathomable. I wondered if the crowd could see it in my walk. It was the witness, one afflicted with all the hurt and burden and grandeur of memory. I wondered if they could see the difference.

No, they saw only a boy who had joined the Line, a boy with a diploma, a smiling happy boy. They saw a boy who would be an Institute man for the rest of his life. A whole man.

They could not see the difference. They did not know their system had proffered me an inestimable gift: It had given me the chance to prove that, though I wore the ring, I was not one of them.

When the ceremony was over, I found the Bear and handed him my diploma along with a ballpoint pen.

"What's this for, lamb?"

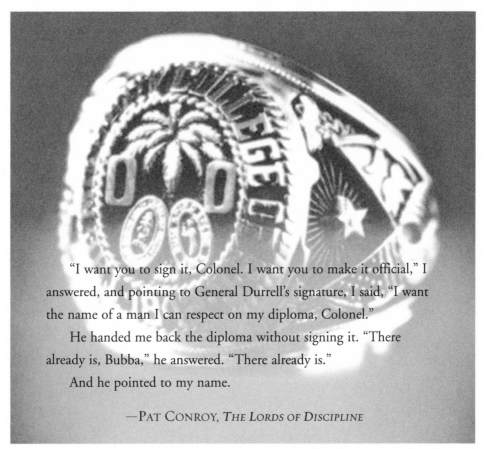

"I want you to sign it, Colonel. I want you to make it official," I answered, and pointing to General Durrell's signature, I said, "I want the name of a man I can respect on my diploma, Colonel."

He handed me back the diploma without signing it. "There already is, Bubba," he answered. "There already is."

And he pointed to my name.

—PAT CONROY, *THE LORDS OF DISCIPLINE*

"Let's hope," I put in, "that Dab-Dab has a nice fire burning in the kitchen."

"I'm sure she will," said the Doctor as he picked out his old handbag from among the bundles. "With this wind from the East she'll need it to keep the animals in the house warm. Come on. Let's hug the riverbank so we don't miss our way in the fog. You know, there's something rather attractive in the bad weather of England—when you've got a kitchen fire to look forward to. . . . Four o'clock! Come along—we'll just be in nice time for tea."

—HUGH LOFTING, *THE VOYAGES OF DOCTOR DOLITTLE*

I follow him up the steps to his building, climbing over the ghost of me from last night, up to his apartment on the top floor. Jezebel and I wait outside while he closes the cat in his bedroom. Then he leads us to his study, which has big dormer windows, all of them open, facing the backyard. He asks if I want a glass of wine, and I say yes.

One wall is covered with taped-up cartoons in black ink and watercolor. I find the gallery of scents from my dog museum. Sea horses bobbing. I see cartoon him, up there pining for cartoon me.

He hands me my wine. And I tell him that his cartoons are beautiful and funny and sad and true.

He smiles.

I ask him what else the review of his dreams says about him. He likes this question. He thinks. Then he says, "Robert Wexler is a goofball in search of truth."

I think, *I'm a truthball in search of goof,* and I realize that I can say whatever I want now. And I do.

Instead of laughing, he pulls me in. We kiss, we kiss, we kiss, in front of Jezebel and all the cartoons. There is no stopping now. Both of us are hunters and prey, fishers and fish. We are the surf 'n' turf special with fries and slaw. We are just two mayflies mating on a summer night.

—MELISSA BANK, *THE GIRLS' GUIDE TO HUNTING AND FISHING*

*B*ut he is not always alone. When the long winter nights come on and the wolves follow their meat into the lower valleys, he may be seen running at the head of the pack through the pale moonlight or glimmering borealis, leaping gigantic above his fellows, his great throat a-bellow as he sings a song of the younger world, which is the song of the pack.

—JACK LONDON, *THE CALL OF THE WILD*

*P*amela stood up, with a large beautifully wrapped parcel in her hand, and walked towards me. I rose at her approach. She was a striking figure as she came proudly up with the parcel, but no sooner had I received it from her hand than she suddenly turned and ran back to her seat to hide her face behind the lid of her desk. At a moment when she so wanted to be at her grown-up best, childhood had claimed her again.

I thanked them and sat down quickly, as the door opened and Mr. Florian walked quietly in; he had been attracted by the noise of cheering. Together we looked at the large label pasted on the parcel and inscribed:

TO SIR,

WITH LOVE

and underneath, the signatures of all of them.

He looked at me and smiled. And I looked over his shoulder at them—my children.

—E. R. BRAITHWAITE, *To Sir, With Love*

"Look there," he said, "if tha's curious. Look what's comin' across th' grass."

When Mrs. Medlock looked she threw up her hands and gave a little shriek and every man and woman servant within hearing bolted across the servants' hall and stood looking through the window with their eyes almost starting out of their heads.

Across the lawn came the Master of Misselthwaite and he looked as many of them had never seen him. And by his side with his head up in the air and his eyes full of laughter walked as strongly and steadily as any boy in Yorkshire—

Master Colin!

—Frances Hodgson Burnett, *The Secret Garden*

"... *I* remember how we sat there and pitied and sympathized with these courageous Southern men who had fought for four long and dreary years all so stubbornly, so bravely and so well, and now, whipped, beaten, completely used up, were fully at our mercy—it was pitiful, sad, hard, and seemed to us altogether too bad." A Pennsylvanian in the V Corps dodged past the skirmish line and strolled into the lines of the nearest Confederate regiment, and half a century after the war he recalled it with a glow: ". . . as soon as I got among these boys I felt and was treated as well as if I had been among our own boys, and a person would of thought we were of the same Army and had been Fighting under the Same Flag."

Down by the roadside near Appomattox Court House, Sheridan and Ord and other officers sat and waited while a brown-bearded little man in a mud-spattered uniform rode up. They all saluted him, and there was a quiet interchange of greetings, and then General Grant tilted his head toward the village and asked: "Is General Lee up there?"

Sheridan replied that he was, and Grant said: "Very well. Let's go up."

The little cavalcade went trotting along the road to the village, and all around them the two armies waited in silence. As the generals neared the end of their ride, a Yankee band in a field near the town struck up "Auld Lang Syne."

—BRUCE CATTON, *A STILLNESS AT APPOMATTOX*

The night was hazy. There was no moon. Farmhouse windows burned with a soft buttery light, as if they were under water. We went from farmland to forest and then picked up the river and followed the river into the mountains. I looked at the country we passed through with a lordly eye, allowing myself small stirrings of fondness for what I thought had failed to hold me. I did not know that the word *home* would forever after be filled with this place.

The air grew clearer as we climbed, and colder. The curves followed fast on one another as the road took the snaky shape of the river. We could see the moon now, a thin silver moon swinging between the black treetops overhead. Chuck kept losing the radio station. Finally he turned off the radio, and we sang Buddy Holly songs for a while. When we got tired of those, we sang hymns. First we sang "I Walk to the Garden Alone" and "The Old Rugged Cross," and a few other quiet ones, just to find our range and get in the spirit. Then we sang the roof-raisers. We sang them with respect and we sang them hard, swaying from side to side and dipping our shoulders in counterpoint. Between hymns we drank from the bottle. Our voices were strong. It was a good night to sing and we sang for all we were worth, as if we'd been saved.

—Tobias Wolff, *This Boy's Life*

So Mr. Wonka and Grandpa Joe and Charlie, taking no notice of their screams, simply pushed the bed into the elevator. They pushed Mr. and Mrs. Bucket in after it. Then they got in themselves. Mr. Wonka pressed a button. The doors closed. Grandma Georgina screamed. And the elevator rose up off the floor and shot through the hole in the roof, out into the open sky.

Charlie climbed onto the bed and tried to calm the three old people who were still petrified with fear. "Please don't be frightened," he said. "It's quite safe. And we're going to the most wonderful place in the world!"

"Charlie's right," said Grandpa Joe.

"Will there be anything to eat when we get there?" asked Grandma Josephine. "I'm starving! The whole family is starving!"

"Anything to *eat*?" cried Charlie, laughing. "Oh, you just wait and see!"

—ROALD DAHL, *CHARLIE AND THE CHOCOLATE FACTORY*

Taken all in all, the sky is a miraculous achievement. . . . It breathes for us, and it does another thing for our pleasure. Each day, millions of meteorites fall against the outer limits of the membrane and are burned to nothing by the friction. Without this shelter, our surface would long since have become the pounded powder of the moon. Even though our receptors are not sensitive enough to hear it, there is comfort in knowing that the sound is there overhead, like the random noise of rain on the roof at night.

—LEWIS THOMAS, *THE LIVES OF A CELL*

April 16. Away! Away!

The spell of arms and voices: the white arms of roads, their promise of close embraces and the black arms of tall ships that stand against the moon, their tale of distant nations. They are held out to say: We are alone—come. And the voices say with them: We are your kinsmen. And the air is thick with their company as they call to me, their kinsman, making ready to go, shaking the wings of their exultant and terrible youth.

April 26. Mother is putting my new secondhand clothes in order. She prays now, she says, that I may learn in my own life and away from home and friends what the heart is and what it feels. Amen. So be it. Welcome, O life! I go to encounter for the millionth time the reality of experience and to forge in the smithy of my soul the uncreated conscience of my race.

April 27. Old father, old artificer, stand me now and ever in good stead.

—JAMES JOYCE, *A PORTRAIT OF THE ARTIST AS A YOUNG MAN*

Daddy said, "I'll tell you what we'll do. We'll all join hands and solemnly pledge that there shall be no more quarreling in this house. Then, we'll all walk up to Findley's Drugstore and seal the pledge with ice cream. Does everyone agree?"

"We all agree," they shouted. So they joined hands and said, "I do solemnly pledge that I will not quarrel or fight in this house ever again."

Then they walked up to Mr. Findley's drugstore and had ice cream sodas and even though Anne saw Mr. Findley put three scoops of ice cream in Joan's soda and only two in hers and even though Joan saw Mr. Findley put two scoops of strawberry in Anne's soda and only one in hers, they neither of them said a word. The Fighter-Quarreleritis was cured.

—BETTY MACDONALD, MRS. PIGGLE-WIGGLE

*T*hey were flying over lush, rolling countryside, with his own blue mountains to the right. He thought it might be the most beautiful thing he had seen in a very long time.

There was a peaceful farm with acres of green crops laid out in neat parcels, and a tractor moving along the road. There was a lake that mirrored the clouds, and the blue sky, and the shadow of the little plane as it passed overhead.

Away toward the mountains, there was a ribbon of water flung out on the land, glittering in the sunlight, and beyond the river, a small, white church with a steeple catching the brilliance of the sun.

He closed the folder in his lap.

"Go in new life," came unbidden to his mind.

He felt as if he were emerging from a long, narrow hallway, from a cocoon, perhaps. He felt a weight lifting off his shoulders as the little plane lifted its gleaming wings over the fields.

Go in new life with Christ, he said silently, wondering at the strangely familiar thought.

Go, and be as the butterfly.

—Jan Karon, *At Home in Mitford*

"Well—" Babbitt crossed the floor, slowly, ponderously, seeming a little old. "I've always wanted you to have a college degree." He meditatively stamped across the floor again. "But I've never— Now, for heaven's sake, don't repeat this to your mother, or she'd remove what little hair I've got left, but practically, I've never done a single thing I've wanted to in my whole life! I don't know 's I've accomplished anything except just get along. I figure out I've made about a quarter of an inch out of a possible hundred rods. Well, maybe you'll carry things on further. I don't know. But I do get a kind of sneaking pleasure out of the fact that you knew what you wanted to do and did it. Well, those folks in there will try to bully you, and tame you down. Tell 'em to go to the devil! I'll back you. Take your factory job, if you want to. Don't be scared of the family. No, nor all of Zenith. Nor of yourself, the way I've been. Go ahead, old man! The world is yours!"

Arms around each other's shoulders, the Babbitt men marched into the living-room and faced the swooping family.

—SINCLAIR LEWIS, *BABBITT*

$\mathcal{O}$ne last bit of household lore that has served me in good stead at Sweet Apple came from my friend Angeline Levey, who once had a maid who was neat, efficient and industrious but absolutely adamant about not "working over my head" or washing windows. She said she had never done either and she didn't intend to.

"But what do you do in your own house when the windows get dirty?" Angie asked.

"Mrs. Levey," said the maid, "if they be's so dirty I can't see out the window, I looks out the door."

—CELESTINE SIBLEY, *A PLACE CALLED SWEET APPLE*

*O*n front of her was a huge white circle, bounded by four-foot-high boards. Glinting, dazzling, enchanting ice. She looked at the ice and slowly it revealed itself. The criss-cross patterns of a thousand surface scars, the colors that shifted and changed in the lights, the unchanging nature of what lay beneath. A woman swooped by on one leg. No sequins, no short skirt. She wore jeans. She raced on, on two legs.

"Here are your boots, Amma."

Nazneen turned around. To get on the ice physically—it hardly seemed to matter. In her mind she was already there.

She said, "But you can't skate in a sari."

Razia was already lacing her boots. "This is England," she said. "You can do whatever you like."

—MONICA ALI, BRICK LANE

When Jim opened his eyes, he saw Uncle Zeno's face swimming inches from his own. Uncle Al and Uncle Coran knelt on either side of him.

"Hey, hey, shh," Uncle Zeno said. "What's the matter?"

Jim waved an arm out at the world beyond the end of the mountain.

Uncle Zeno frowned and shook his head.

"It's too big," Jim said.

"What is?"

"Everything."

"I don't understand, Doc."

"I'm just a boy," he said.

Uncle Zeno rocked back on his heels. He looked at Uncle Coran and Uncle Al, then smiled at Jim.

"We know that," he said. "But you're *our* boy."

—TONY EARLEY, *JIM THE BOY*

*C*lay felt the peace about him, the peace glowing in Nat. "Do you remember," he asked, his voice hardly above a whisper, "years ago you told me how you used to feel God on nights like this? Do you now?"

"Yes—sometimes. It's different. I'm not a boy any more, but I feel something beautiful that's God to me."

"Farmer, father, husband, friend," Clay murmured. "That's all you want to be, isn't it, Nat?"

Nat looked at him and drew a deep breath. He looked at the house, his house, the windows shining now with light. His wife was there, his mother—and his son. There were the mountains and the river, the rich fertile fields, the sturdy animals in the barn, over the ridge Tom and Molly and their children.

"Say that again," he demanded urgently. "What was it? Farmer, father—"

"Farmer, father," Clay repeated, "husband, friend. It seems to me that's all you want to be.

Nat placed his big, hard hand on Clay's shoulder. "Yes, that's all I want to be." He smiled. "That's enough, isn't it?"

—PERCY MARKS, *WHAT'S A HEAVEN FOR?*

*E*ppie had a larger garden than she had ever expected there now; and in other ways there had been alterations at the expense of Mr. Cass, the landlord, to suit Silas's larger family. For he and Eppie had declared that they would rather stay at the Stone Pits than go to any new home. The garden was fenced with stones on two sides, but in front there was an open fence, through which the flowers shone with answering gladness, as the four united people came within sight of them.

"Oh, Father," said Eppie, "what a pretty home ours is! I think nobody could be happier than we are."

—GEORGE ELIOT, *SILAS MARNER*

*D*ear Aunt Polly and Uncle Tom:

Oh, I can—I can—I *can* walk! I did today all the way from my bed to the window! It was six steps. My, how good it was to be on legs again!

All the doctors stood around and smiled, and all the nurses stood beside of them and cried. A lady in the next ward who walked last week first, peeked into the door, and another one who hopes she can walk next month, was invited in to the party, and she laid on my nurse's bed and clapped her hands. Even Black Tilly who washes the floor, looked through the piazza window and called me "Honey, child" when she wasn't crying too much to call me anything.

I don't see why they cried. *I* wanted to sing and shout and yell! Oh—oh—oh! Just think, I can walk—walk—*walk!* Now I don't mind being here almost ten months, and I didn't miss the wedding, anyhow. Wasn't that just like you, Aunt Polly, to come on here and get married right beside my bed, so I could see you. You always do think of the gladdest things!

Pretty soon, they say, I shall go home. I wish I could walk all the way there. I do. I don't think I shall ever want to ride anywhere any more. It will be so good just to walk. Oh, I'm so glad! I'm glad for everything. Why, I'm glad now I lost my legs for a while, for you never, never know how perfectly lovely legs are till you haven't got them— that go, I mean. I'm going to walk eight steps tomorrow.

With heaps of love to everybody,

Pollyanna

—ELEANOR H. PORTER, *POLLYANNA*

I hear cars coming down off the main road, right about dusk it is, so I get up from my comfortable spot, put on my shoes and coat, and go out to greet the family as they come in. I want to greet them with a greeting that's big like the Christmas quilt star is big, one that says, "Love lives here." So I go out the front door, and I stand on the front porch. I see them all coming down the road, the tires of the cars making little tracks. Danged if it hasn't been snowing while I sat reminiscing. And I look around, and I figure it's not such a bad thing after all, one small flake following another, settling on the ground soft like a kiss from heaven, covering Smoky Hollow like a blanket of grace that shines white with goodness.

—THOMAS J. DAVIS, *THE CHRISTMAS QUILT*

"Hold your tongue!" said the Queen, turning purple.

"I won't!" said Alice.

"Off with her head!" the Queen shouted at the top of her voice. Nobody moved.

"Who cares for *you*?" said Alice (she had grown to her full size by this time). "You're nothing but a pack of cards!"

At this the whole pack rose up into the air, and came flying down upon her; she gave a little scream, half of fright and half of anger, and tried to beat them off, and found herself lying on the bank, with her head in the lap of her sister, who was gently brushing away some dead leaves that had fluttered down from the trees upon her face.

"Wake up, Alice dear!" said her sister. "Why, what a long sleep you've had!"

"Oh, I've had such a curious dream!" said Alice. And she told her sister, as well as she could remember them, all these strange Adventures

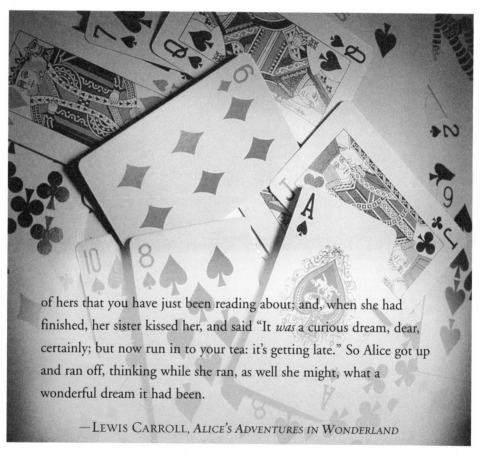

of hers that you have just been reading about; and, when she had finished, her sister kissed her, and said "It *was* a curious dream, dear, certainly; but now run in to your tea: it's getting late." So Alice got up and ran off, thinking while she ran, as well she might, what a wonderful dream it had been.

—LEWIS CARROLL, *ALICE'S ADVENTURES IN WONDERLAND*

*H*ave you ever really had a teacher? One who saw you as a raw but precious thing, a jewel that, with wisdom, could be polished to a proud shine? If you are lucky enough to find your way to such teachers, you will always find your way back. Sometimes it is only in your head. Sometimes it is right alongside their beds.

The last class of my old professor's life took place once a week, in his home, by a window in his study where he could watch a small hibiscus plant shed its pink flowers. The class met on Tuesdays. No books were required. The subject was the meaning of life. It was taught from experience.

The teaching goes on.

—MITCH ALBOM, *TUESDAYS WITH MORRIE*

5

Tuesday
May

7:00	
7:30	
8:00	
8:30	
9:00	
9:30	
10:00	
10:30	
11:00	
11:30	
12:00	
12:30	
1:00	
1:30	
2:00	

"There *was* a real railway accident," said Aslan softly. "Your father and mother and all of you are—as you used to call it in the Shadowlands—dead. The term is over: the holidays have begun. The dream is ended: this is the morning."

And as He spoke He no longer looked to them like a lion; but the things that began to happen after that were so great and beautiful that I cannot write them. And for us this is the end of all the stories, and we can most truly say that they all lived happily ever after. But for them it was only the beginning of the real story. All their life in this world and all their adventures in Narnia had only been the cover and the title page: now at last they were beginning Chapter One of the Great Story which no one on earth has read: which goes on forever: in which every chapter is better than the one before.

—C. S. LEWIS, *THE LAST BATTLE*

AND THEY ALL LIVED

Happily Ever After . . .

Acknowledgments

For permission to reprint copyrighted material, grateful acknowledgment is made to the following publishers, authors, and agents.

Book jacket and page 6, from *The Hobbit* by J. R. R. Tolkien. Copyright © 1966 by J. R. R. Tolkien. Copyright © renewed 1994 by Christopher R. Tolkien, John F. R. Tolkien, and Priscilla M. A. R. Tolkien. Reprinted by permission of Houghton Mifflin Company. All rights reserved.

Page 8, from *Little House in the Big Woods* by Laura Ingalls Wilder. Published by HarperCollins. Text copyright © 1932, 1960 by Little House Heritage Trust.

Page 10, from "A Pair of Tickets," *The Joy Luck Club* by Amy Tan, copyright © 1989 by Amy Tan. Used by permission of G. P. Putnam's Sons, a division of Penguin Group (USA) Inc.

Page 16, reprinted with the permission of Scribner, an imprint of Simon & Schuster Adult Publishing Group. From *Angela's Ashes* by Frank McCourt. Copyright © 1996 by Frank McCourt.

Page 22, from *Lake Wobegon Days* by Garrison Keillor, copyright © 1985 by Garrison Keillor. Used by permission of Viking Penguin, a division of Penguin Group (USA) Inc.

Photograph Credits

Pages vi, 3, 7, 11, 13, 15, 17, 19, 21, 23, 25, 35, 37, 39, 41, 43, 47, 49, 51, 53, 57, 59, 61, 63, 65, 67, 69, 71, 73, 75, 79, 81, 83, 89, 91, 93, 97, 103, 105, 109, 113, 115, 119, 121, 123, 125, 127, 129, 131, Picturequest.

Pages 5, 27, 33, 77, 99, 101, 107, Getty Images.

Page 9, courtesy of Laura Ingalls Wilder Home Association, Mansfield, MO (photo by Phillip Bennett).

Page 29, Digital Vision.

Pages 31, 117, Photodisc.

Pages 45, 55, 85, 87, 95, Carl Jones.

Page 111, FotoSearch.